THE ADVENTURES AND CONQUESTS OF ELLIE THE ELEPHANT SHREW

FIVE SHORT STORIES

Tugbiyele, Hazel

Adventures & conquests of Ellie the elephant shrew/ Hazel Tugbiyele – 1st ed.

ISBN 978-1-365-09764-5

9 781365 097645

Printed in the United States of America

First edition, May 2016

SPECIAL THANKS TO:

God, because without him I could never had found someone to publish my book, found people to help me write, nor found people who shared my interests and were a great encouragement.

My sixth grade science class for encouraging me and giving me ideas to write this first book.

My tutors at *Huntington Learning Center*, Amanda and Hillary, for giving me writing pointers and guiding me through the extensive writing process.

Paula, the director at *Huntington Learning Center*, for offering to read my work before publish date.

My family, for showing interest in my gift and helping me to continue writing.

AUTHOR'S NOTE

I first got the idea for this book back in 2015 during a science class. My teacher introduced me and my class to an animal called *Rufous sengi,* or more commonly known as, the elephant shrew.

Having a writer's mind as most budding authors do, I decided to write a book on the queer animal, but this time, I was hoping to get my writing out to the real world instead of hoarding my work as usual.

I started writing. A task that I had long taken care of prior to this book was securing a publisher. I had thought that my publisher would be a person who would have to approve my book and contact me through hundreds of long, professional emails. I did not know, however, that my publisher would come in the form of a website known as lulu.com. I do recommend the website and suggest you check it out.

I had also started attending a tutoring program called Huntington Learning Center around the time I was first introduced to this new character and was beginning to develop her. I had, and still have, amazing tutors to work with me on this project.

Amanda and Hillary have been awesome. Hillary taught me to have a reader's mind as well as a writer's mind, thinking about what the reader would like to hear in the next chapter, not what I would necessarily like to write. Amanda worked with me primarily on this book and for their help I am very grateful.

I hope you enjoy this book and my other works of literature that you may see. I want to touch the world with wonderful stories that have a purpose and through my writing encourage and enlighten people for the higher purpose that God has set out for them.

Happy Reading,

Brooklyn Citifaire

STORIES INCLUDED

ABOUT THE ELEPHANT SHREW

Ellie is an elephant shrew, a species native to Africa. Its native name is Rufous Sengi, and it is related to species like aardvarks, hyraxes, sea cows, and even elephants. The minute mammal must learn to survive underfoot of some extremely massive animals.

The key to Ellie's survival, and the survival of her town, is their network of tunnels. Unlike Ellie and her friends, elephant shrews only spend about 2-3 minutes resting. Most of their time is spent eating and making tunnels.

Elephant shrews make their tunnels by biting off grass, twigs and leaves that might block their path while running. They also sweep out their tunnels using their legs and forehead, as mentioned in the story *Ellie Battles Emerson Eagle*.

Elephant shrew's legs are also good for leaping as well as running. A shrew can jump over three times its body length. As mentioned in *Ellie Battles Emerson Eagle* and *Ellie Defeats Lord Lizard,* Ellie uses her leaping powers to get up to high places, usually during a battle with an evil predator.

Elephant shrew's diets consist of insects, as mentioned several times in the story. Readers will always catch Ellie eating, for elephant shrews spend quite a lot of time eating during their day.

Shrews learn their talents by instinct and these amazing adaptations, autonomy, orderliness, and agility, allows them to thrive in the African savannas.

ELLIE BATTLES EMERSON EAGLE

Across the plains of Africa, a young elephant shrew helped her mother clean out tunnels. This young elephant shrew, named Ellie, was but a simple girl by day, but also a daring superhero by night.

"Ellie," her mother called to her. "If you see an eagle, do warn me. I will be inside preparing our lunch."

Ellie knew very well that there had been only one eagle who continued to return to harm Shrewlandia each night. His name was Emerson, and he was a hungry eagle with wild matted feathers. Rumor had it that he was in exile with his wife, Helena, and his son, Maximus, and he was trying his best to provide for them.

The people of Shrewlandia were hardworking peasants who hunted for insects and lived off the surroundings. Most of the young boys and girls were in Insect Hunters Academy, training to become great hunters and bring honor and glory to the little village society.

Ellie knew very well how much her mother and father wanted her to succeed in hunting, as finding food was crucial to the shrews with the amount of fleeing that they did. Every second, one could find them eating yet another helping of Beans and Beetle Stew.

Ellie shook her head. "No thanks Mom! I'll be heading to the Insect Gourmet with Maddie and Annie. And you *know* I'll be on the lookout for eagles!"

Ellie took off to the Insect Gourmet to meet her best friends Maddie and Annie. They were adventurous shrews who dreamed of life outside the humble, run-down town of Shrewlandia with its meager portions of insect delicacies. They wanted to be the ones battling eagles and snakes and lizards instead of running and hiding in their burrows.

"So," asked Maddie once Ellie had pulled herself up to the spinning barstool by the cooking counter. "What're you going to order?" Ellie shrugged and glanced at the menu. Everything was tasty there from the Beetle Bacon Burgers to the scorpion soups. "I think I'll just get the scorpion soup with a side of chopped centipede." Ellie announced.

"Good," Maddie approved as the waiter removed their menus from the table. "I ordered a beetle burger, no bacon, with millipede milk." Annie hopped onto a barstool next to them. "Hey guys!" she said.

The girls ate and talked. Every so often Ellie glanced at the window to see if Emerson was flying about overhead. As the girls sprinted out into the sunshine and walked over to the main tunnel that ran through the village, a sudden shriek echoed through the air.

It's Emerson, Ellie thought as she and her friends continued to run down the tunneled path. *And if I don't stop him, he's going to take a Shrewlandian citizen for dinner.*

Back in her burrow, Ellie washed and dried her superhero cape, boots, and hat. She fixed her superhero watch. She raced the network of tunnels in Shrewlandia to put a fresh copy in her brain. She had amazing powers, like Super Shrew Memory, Super Shrew Speed, and Super Shrew Leaps.

That night, Emerson's shriek rang out across the African plains. *Ayyyeeeahh!* The unmistakable call of the eagle clan. It meant: *Get up! It's time to eat!*

Ellie pulled a tree branch lever and the ground opened up to reveal her secret superhero base. She rode down the little elevator and put on her superhero costume. Her cape blew in the windy base. It read, *The Amazing Ellie the Elephant Shrew! Challenge if you dare.*

Ellie knew that only desperate animals, like Emerson, and only foolish birdbrains, like Lord Lizard or Sinister Snake, would try to challenge her. Other villains, she sent running home with their tail between their legs.

Ellie leaped out into the silent night. In her mind, she pictured the network of tunnels that led around Shrewlandia. Ten different hiding spots were pinpointed. "Perfect," she told herself. "Now to stop Emerson."

Emerson had been a well-known business bird until he cheated his job by using their money to sell products to other companies in secret. He and his newly wed eagle, Helena, were forced to leave Staten Eagle. They found a tree to nest in and their son, Maximus, was born. Now Emerson was trying to provide for the sickly baby bird and his wife was trying so hard to make Maximus stronger.

Ellie knew this from her days of spying on newcomers, since Emerson had once been a trading partner for Shrewlandia. But once in exile, he made his partners into dinner, blaming them for his troubles. "If only you were fair with trade!" he often told them.

The shriek rang out again. Emerson quickly spotted his first meal, having superior eyesight and all. He dove for the kill. Catching Ellie would be easy if only.....she'd stay still!

Ellie dodged, twisted and turned corners as fast as she could. Her cape flew up into the air as a symbol of her bravery and perseverance. Long had she waited for this moment, to be able to finally send Emerson on the run.

Up and down, right and left, she sprinted past the homes in the village, where everyone had their little leaf curtains down, comforting young ones who might be scared that they would be eaten or fed to other eagles.

Ellie finally reached the safe hiding spot. "Super Shrew Leap!" Her power activated with a crackle and a fizz and she jumped into that hole. Emerson poked around with his beak for a few moments, but then he flew off into the night. Ellie could hear the cries of confusion and disappointment coming from his little yellow beak. Soon he was just a speck in the moonlight.

The citizens proclaimed that they would award the great superhero for her bravery and for saving them, but she was off into the night. Maddie and Annie tried to chase her but she disappeared into her secret base before they could catch her. When she came up again, she was a regular Ellie, content and proud.

Maddie and Annie stood outside her burrow. "Ellie, great Shrewlandia! You missed the brave hero who chased off that eagle! Why, she even disappeared into your burrow!" Ellie pounced on a beetle like she didn't hear. "Maddie,

Annie, you should really go back to bed." She yawned for added effect, then disappeared into her burrow. Maddie and Annie shrugged, a little confused.

Ellie climbed into her bed and pulled the covers over her head. "Another villain, another hero," she said, and drifted off to sleep.

ELLIE DEFEATS LORD LIZARD

Maddie, Ellie and Annie were helping to clean Ellie's mother's burrow. Annie swept the cockroaches off the bed, Ellie roasted them, and Maddie made the bed again. They were a good time, stopping only to gaze at Gertie as she whistled and walked to the Shrew Discount Mart.

Finally, the curiosity was too strong. The girls hurried over to Gertie and stopped her. "Good Gertie," Maddie asked, "Would you be so kind as to tell us why you're whistling?" Gertie grinned a big grin. "I got a coupon in the mail for the *Extra Special Deluxe Pack* of *Insectoid Trail Mix!*"

Ellie screamed! Maddie screamed! Annie screamed! The girls all begged Gertie to let them walk with her to the Mart. "We want to buy the ESDPITM! We must buy it!" Gertie's face scrunched in confusion. "What's ESDPITM?" Annie slapped her forehead. "Duh! Extra special deluxe pack insectoid trail mix!"

Gertie and the girls hurried to the Shrew Discount Mart to buy the trail mix. As they entered the store, Ellie heard a sound that sounded an awful lot like a lizard creeping around. "I heard a lizard!" Ellie told Maddie, but Maddie rolled her eyes. "No you didn't, you scared shrew." Maddie shot back in annoyance as she picked up a bag of trail mix and walked to the checkout counter.

Annie and Ellie headed to the back of the store. "We're going to buy some cosmetic items." Annie pretended to faint. "I often faint at the horrific sight of my fur." Ellie and the others laughed. "I just need some Fresh Fur Lotion and Paula's Paw Putty."

As Ellie reached up to grab a carton of the lotion, she heard a squeal. "It's a lizard!" someone shouted. Ellie and Annie raced to the front. Gertie was frozen with fear and Maddie was hiding in a storage closet. The other customers were fleeing and the store manager was being pelted in demands for refunds by those who had been shopping.

Ellie snuck behind a shelf and donned her superhero boots and cape. She smothered her last bit of paw putty onto her paws to make her run faster. Then she dashed out to face the scary lizard.

Gertie was running up and down the aisles now. Lord Lizard started after her. Maddie shrieked and pulled Annie into the storage closet with her. The echo of a closing door rang throughout the Mart.

Ellie jerked to a stop in front of Gertie. "Don't touch her!" she commanded Lord Lizard. But that lizard was stubborn! "Lord Lizard listens to no one!" he said. Ellie breathed hard. Smoke shot out of her nostrils. "Well then I'll teach you how to listen!" she roared.

"Super Shrew Leap!" Ellie leaped up onto the back of the horrendous lizard whose only pleasure was to harass her town. She hopped off the other side and began to run down the aisles and out of the double doors. "Come catch me you big old meanie!" she taunted.

Lord Lizard followed slowly. With every step he took, the Mart shook violently, and the customers felt their bones rattling. He roared with anger and he tried his hardest to continue running after the already long gone shrew.

For half an hour Lord Lizard pursued Ellie. Ellie, being so very clever, was able to keep running for this long due to the amount of scorpion soup she was able to drink while she ran. On her helmet was a small pouch of Scorpion Soup. A straw extended down to her mouth. As she ran, she ate. Thus, she had more energy than the bumbling lizard.

For the millionth time Ellie zoomed past the Shrew Discount Mart. For the millionth time Lord Lizard pulled himself past, getting slower with each step. Ellie stopped and looked back. Lord Lizard was sprawled out on Main Street. "Come on you shrew muncher!" Ellie called at him. "Come catch me!"

Lord Lizard opened one of his eyes. Ellie ran over to him. "Lord Lizard?" she asked quietly. Lord Lizard struggled to his feet, gave one last grunt, and hobbled off slowly out of Shrewlandia. He huffed and puffed. Ellie was overjoyed. Mayor Shrew came out of his big mayoral house.

"Again great and honorable hero, you save our small city from harm. I myself would like to reward you with a formal ceremony, for your great deeds have once again…."

Ellie snuck off while the mayor continued his long speech which she knew the townspeople would soon not be interested in. She took of her superhero cape and headed inside the Mart to finish her shopping. Reaching up again to grab a jar of Fresh Fur Lotion and a tin can of Paula's Paw Putty, she smiled brightly.

Ellie walked up to the counter and payed for her items. The cashier talked about the amazing hero who had just saved the town. "Wasn't she great?" the cashier asked earnestly. Ellie nodded, knowing very well how great the hero was.

Outside in the sunshine, Ellie took a long look at her town, and then she said, "Another villain, another hero," and ran to join Maddie, Annie and Gertie out in the town square.

ELLIE TAKES ON
SINISTER SNAKE

Birthdays! Ellie just loved birthdays because they brought everyone together to have big parties and eat lots of food. Ellie's best friend Annie was having a birthday today, and she and Maddie had taken it upon themselves to help to plan a surprise birthday party for her. Even Gertie was helping.

"A little bit to the left!" Maddie called to the shrew on the ladder. Maddie was in charge of the party decorations. She had bought pink streamers, yellow ribbons, orange balloons, and green party cannons; all to find that the room Insect Gourmet was lending them for the party was too small to fit three party cannons. The tables had taken up all the space.

Gertie, the smarter shopper of the girls, had bought the tried-and-true Paula's Paw Putty for party favors. She had a sharp tongue, but she was good at saving coupons so that she didn't pay a cent, and she could buy things to the lowest sales with her bargaining methods. "And," she added as she bagged yet another jar of putty, "I even told the manager that he could forget business if he didn't shrink that price. 'Forty-two cents for a jar of putty is outrageous!' I told him."

Ellie, being a superhero and all, was given the task of making sure no one trashed the party. Ellie herself had volunteered for this job, and in her purse was her superhero gear.

"The delivery man is here!" Ellie announced as Maddie was directing the shrew as to where to put the streamer. "Whoa!" the man fell off the ladder and right into the box of forgotten party cannons. *Toot!* Confetti flew into the air. An orange piece flew into Maddie's open mouth. She coughed it up. Gertie giggled. "Oh Maddie, you really shouldn't have dropped out of the Academy. You learn common sense there too!"

The delivery man came in with a box of millipede milkshakes. "Ellie?" he asked. She ran over. "That's my name, don't wear it out!" Ellie took the box and began unloading the milkshakes for each guest. As she was placing a straw into one of the cups, Gertie tapped her shoulder.

"Listen," Gertie said. "I know your job is keeping obnoxious things out of here, but does Annie count? Because she's coming right toward the Gourmet!" Ellie dropped the cup and rushed outside. Annie looked a little depressed. "Hey Birthday Girl!" Ellie sang. "Why the long face?"

Annie sighed. "You all forgot my birthday," she complained. Ellie cleared her throat. "No we didn't! We're just working on making it extra special." As Ellie patted Annie's shoulder, her cellphone began to ring. "Hey Ellie!" It was Maddie. "Can you come back to the shop? There's something you need to see."

Ellie raced as fast as her little legs would carry her. She dashed through the double doors and looked up. She was face to face with a snake! "Sinister Snake?" she asked, surprised. "I thought I'd-I mean that superhero! I thought she had defeated you!" Sinister cackled. "I never get defeated little shrew. But before the superhero gets here, I'll have already eaten you! Muhahaha!"

She raced outside. Sinister Snake followed close behind. Annie ran up to her. "Ellie! Is the surprise done?" Ellie shook her head. "If I don't catch-I mean if I don't call the superhero, there won't be a surprise!"

Ellie raced behind some grasses. When she was sure Sinister had passed by, she quickly changed into her superhero suit. Leaping out, Ellie quickly began to pursue the evil snake as he slithered through the town.

Citizens cheered as Ellie raced through the town, right on Sinister's heels. Sinister was known for being able to hypnotize his nemeses. Ellie knew this, and having been hypnotized by the rude reptile before, she knew just how to avoid his nasty spells.

To start off, Sinister recited an ancient chant. Ellie, refusing to look at him, recited the counter spell. *Whoosh! Zoom! Ka-pow!* Sinister was out cold. The people cheered. Maddie and Gertie had finished decorating and were watching the brave Ellie.

Sinister slowly rose to his feet. "How dare you combat my special tactic?! You weren't so smart last time!" In spite of herself, Ellie laughed. "You say that all the time. Next time," she added, looking intently at his green scaly face, "I'll be smarter."

Sinister slithered off. He grinned an evil grin. "I'll be back you speedy superhero," he said. Then, he was off. Maddie and Gertie surrounded Ellie and hugged her.

"My goodness, you've done it again!" they cheered. "If only Ellie was here," Gertie said thoughtfully. "I'm sure she'd love to meet you." Ellie nodded and ran off. Soon she was back, but as her regular self. Annie was behind her.

"C'mon Annie," Ellie said. "The girls and I have planned a great surprise for you." Ellie showed Annie the party room. "Happy Birthday Annie!" Maddie congratulated. "The guests should be arriving soon."

Annie was puzzled. "Guests?" "Yes!" Gertie exclaimed. "This is your birthday party after all!" And Annie smiled the biggest smile she'd ever smiled.

THE CRAZY
CONVENTION

Ellie's hands shook with fear and anticipation as she opened the envelope. The International Guild of Superheroes had been writing her letters and recommending training courses to better her powers since she first began to use them. She had participated in the sweepstakes, hoping to win the spot on National Superhero TV as a guest speaker for the First Time Superhero Convention in Staten Eagle.

"Yes!" she squealed. The letter said that she has been chosen as guest speaker 14 for the convention and she would be there for 2 weeks speaking in various conference rooms and all of her expenses would be paid for. "Oh my gosh!" Ellie exclaimed.

As she stepped out of her house to tell Maddie, Annie and Gertie that she'd be out of town for a few days and to watch for her favorite superhero on TV, Maddie came running up to her. "Ellie! Ellie! The school invited us to speak about the importance of fast running at two o'clock tomorrow! Please say you can speak with me and the girls!"

Ellie shook her head. "Gee Maddie, I'm sorry but, I was just asked to speak at an international conference and my train to Staten Eagle is booked for noon tomorrow and…."

Maddie gasped. "Staten Eagle?! Isn't that where the dreaded evil eagle lives? The one that superhero defeated?" Ellie nodded. "I'm not afraid of a little birdie," she announced.

Maddie shook her head. "I'm not sure you want to go there." Ellie shrugged. "Hey, if you watch the National Superhero TV channel like I do, be sure to look for our town's very own savior. She's going to be on I think. There's some convention going on in Staten Eagle. Luckily, I'm not going. Eagles often strike in large crowds. I'm speaking at a smaller event but, fill me in on the superhero!" Ellie hurried off before Maddie could even answer.

Ellie quickly packed for her trip. She took her superhero outfit, watch, boots, and helmet. She packed her soft pajamas from Maddie, with centipede pictures all over it. Maddie was a good seamstress. She packed her trail mix coupons from Gertie, who said that Staten Eaglets liked to shop cheap. She packed her diary and her gold fountain pen from Annie, who often told her to collect souvenirs wherever she went. The fountain pen was from a medieval torture fair.

The next day, Maddie, Annie and Gertie walked with Ellie to the train station. "Be sure to buy lots of memorabilia!" Annie hollered as the train began to huff and puff down the tracks. "Be sure to wear fancy pajamas!" Maddie screamed as the conductor began to fiddle with the controls. "Be sure to shop cheap and bargain hard!" yelled Gertie as the train disappeared out of sight. Each girl sighed sadly.

Ellie's train stopped at New Snake, since she was taking a another train to Colonial Lizard's-burg, and then a train to Staten Eagle. Ellie, quite exhausted from the rickety train, stopped at a buffet in the station to eat. It was then that she noticed someone very familiar in the restaurant. He seemed to know her.

The mysterious animal slithered onto a barstool next to Ellie. He ordered a plated of stuffed mouse and egg tart. Then he turned to Ellie. 'I've been waiting for you," he said. Ellie jumped. "I'm sorry," she quickly apologized. "You startled me there."

The animal, which Ellie soon realized was a snake, continued. "I know all about you Ellie the Elephant Shrew. You are a well-known superhero." Ellie was perplexed. *How does this creep know me? Unless.....*

Ellie jumped from the chair. "Sinister!" she announced. The snake hopped off his chair. "Excellent guess my furry fiend. But I am not going to challenge you today, no-ho-ho! I just want to see the look on your face when I tell you that you won't be showing your face at that convention." Ellie blinked as if she hadn't even heard him.

Sinister scratched his head. "Huh, that was not the reaction I expected. Never mind," he said, "I have to catch a train to Colonial Lizard's-burg to meet up with Lord Lizard. He and I are responsible for preventing you from getting to Staten Eagle. Emerson is already there causing a ruckus for the new heroes."

Sinister laughed and slithered out of the store. An elderly frog came next to her and sat on the chair Sinister had been sitting. Ellie looked at him with a blaze of fire in her eyes. "I wouldn't sit there," she warned, "Unless you want your butt on pure evil." The frog shook his head. "You kids are gettin' stranger every day!" he remarked.

Ellie dashed from the buffet. The train to Lizard's-burg had just arrived in the station. She slipped onto one of the seats. Looking out the window, she noticed Sinister trying to figure out which bus to get on. *That's it!* she thought. "Super Shrew Speed!" Ellie zoomed from her seat, switched the signs on the train, and zoomed right back on.

A little girl-chicken, who had been about to take her seat right where Ellie had been sitting, was quite surprised when she landed on the lap of an elephant shrew. "Eww!" she shrieked. "Mommy!" Ellie chuckled to herself as Sinister boarded the train that read, "Colonial Lizard's-burg." But he really was boarding a train to Lan-cow-ster!

As Ellie arrived in Lizard's-burg she was greeted by a nasty surprise. "Hello Ellie." She whirled around to find herself face to face with Lord Lizard. Sinister was right behind him. "Thought you could trick me with your little train game?" he asked, huffing and puffing.

Ellie hurried away. Sinister and Lord were right behind her. "Whoa!" she darted this way and that. Sprinting past a few scattered stores, she remembered Gerties warning about cheap shopping. *I have an idea!* she thought.

Ellie slowed down and walked casually into a French couture store. It was called: Mama de France. The saleslady had a thick accent that was hard to understand. "Hallo friend! Has you come to shop today, *oui*?!" Ellie couldn't speak any French, so she answered, "I have come to shop today, yes, *oui*."

Hiding in the racks of expensive jewelry, Ellie scanned the windows. She watched Lord Lizard and Sinister Snake peer through the windows of each store. As they neared Mama de France, Ellie hurried to the Employees Only door and shut herself inside it.

Ellie listened to make sure the coast was clear before opening the door and running out of the French store. "I see you later, yes?" the woman asked. Ellie didn't answer, but only nodded.

Outside, it began to rain. "I can't believe that I was just chased by the two most evil villains I know!" She shuddered and returned to the train station, only to find that she had been away too long and that the train to Staten Eagle had departed.

Sitting on a cold bench in the empty station, Ellie thought about what to do. Finally, she told the ticket master that she needed to be in Staten Eagle tomorrow and that she needed the next possible train ride to the large metropolis.

"All large cities are closed. No more trains going to Staten or New Snake until tomorrow, and I think Staten's getting a lot of trains lately. Some superhero convention. Anyway, there's a little mine town that houses a mix of animals about your size. They can take you there tonight on their little coal wagon and ship you in Staten first thing tomorrow."

"Thank you!" Ellie squealed excitedly. She waited for the coal miners to arrive at the station. While the ticket master talked to a big, bluff miner, she talked to a smaller miner who gladly agreed to let her ride with them on the wagon.

"And that's you solve a problem with twists, turns and upside downs!" Ellie concluded her speech at the First Time Superhero Convention. "I'm so glad to be here in Staten Eagle and I really think that every hero should be bilingual."

The Guild's President congratulated her afterward. "Wow Ellie! I heard all about your story from the coal miners. You really made it a commitment to get here…..well anyway, I wanted to ask you if you'd like to be part of the Guild. It's a great way to receive expertise training and live with the big shots. You want your talents to be recognized, right?"

Ellie thought a moment. Did she want to be part of a big shot superhero team? Or did she want to live a life in a small town that was full of illiterate shrews who wanted to fill their bellies? What did she want for herself?

Finally she answered, "No thank you sir. This has been great and all, but, as soon as it's all over, I just want to go home to my friends. They're enough. Besides, there's a need for heroes back home."

And that's just what she did.

THE UNEXPECTED THIEF

Number one! Sit up tall and keep eye contact.

Number two! Give your hopes for this job, make sure they know that you'll learn anything they teach you, and don't mention that you're a school drop-out. They will never let you work if they know that.

Ellie reviewed her rules as she sat outside the office. She was waiting to be interviewed for the job at Insect Gourmet as chief of menu management. She would be the one to write the menus and change the styles and pick the soup of the day. She loved soup.

"Next! Ellie the Elephant Shrew? Oh yes, there you are sweetie! Come on in! Mr. Gourmet Shrew is waiting."

Ellie walked in to the office. "I'm Ellie and I…."

"Hold it! Don't talk till you're talked to Ms. the Elephant Shrew." A short stubby shrew came out and sat on a swivel chair. Ellie smiled sweetly. She waved and waited. Mr. Gourmet cleared his throat and said, "Hello Ms. the Elephant Shrew. I understand you're applying for the position of *a la de carte de menu* yes?"

Ellie, a little confused by the man who was to soon be her boss, only nodded. "Speak when you are spoken too!" Mr. Gourmet commanded. Ellie nodded again. "I'm sorry."

Mr. Gourmet asked very pointed questions that required detailed and descriptive answers. Finally he said, "Thank you for your time Ms. the Elephant Shrew! We look forward to you patronizing us here at Insect Gourmet. However, a work position here may not be for you."

Disappointed, Ellie went home to call her friends. As she stepped through the doorway of her burrow, she found Maddie, Annie, and Gertie slouched against her chairs and bed. "Bad job interviews too?" she asked. All three girls nodded. "Mmm-hmmm."

Maddie spoke first. "I love sewing, I'm very good, and you've seen my sewing! But this shrew is very particular. She knits, not sews. Huh! I should've read the sign, Button's Knitting Shop, before I applied. I didn't get the job. Who wants to work with a fussy, one-track minded boss?"

Annie had less trouble, but her interview still was horrible. "I'm telling you!" she said, "That man doesn't have a mind for my travel brochures. Annie's Travel Brochures are from all over. He'll get more vacay planning business if he has travel brochures. It's $15 for him to own a pack of 6 brochures, not too expensive considering the cost of the brochure in the place I got it."

Gertie had the least trouble of all. "I nearly got the job," she admitted. "But they're trying to start a Shrew Discount Mart in Bat-lehem, so they need workers for that market. I told them to employ bats. There's no way I'm leaving my friends to work in night-time town!"

Ellie sighed. "The Gourmet owner is too Socratic. He asks pointed questions with one-track answers. I don't have a strict salary! I don't bunk with a friend! I certainly am not married! What in the name of Shrewlandia is that nonsense?"

The girls slept over at Ellie's for the night. The next day, Ellie had a plan. "Why not open our own stores? What we want, how we want it! If no one will take us, then we'll....well we'll start our own businesses!"

Within a week, Sew Simple had 100 customers, and most of them were from big cities like Bat-lehem, Staten Eagle, and Lan-cow-ster. And in that same week, Top Travels had 80 customers also from the biggest cities in the Animal Lands. Another business, Compound Groceries, was getting more customers than the 30-year-long Shrew Discount Mart!

Only Ellie was still job-less as she visited her friend's stores, buying well sewn hats and scarves, buying Beetle and Bean stew from Compound Groceries, and listening to Annie's travel lectures for $3. And her friends didn't try to employ her.

At home all alone, she suddenly heard a loud shriek from across town. A hooded figure was sneaking out of Maddie's store. Ellie put on her superhero outfit and ran to confront the thief.

The thief dashed away. Ellie followed, right on his heels, pursuing the culprit. He turned a corner and then disappeared. Ellie soon found herself in a misty, dirty alleyway behind a few businesses that relied on gas and oil to power their appliances.

"Ah-hah!" a creepy voice suddenly called. In the shadowy alley, it was impossible to see who was making the sound. Ellie turned around and around constantly, preparing for an attack. The shadow wielded a sword.

Ellie dodged his first blow, sliding under his open legs and hurrying out of the alley. She climbed up a side wall and hid under the straw beds on the roof. The thief circled the store she was hiding in. "Where are you?!" he shouted. Ellie fought the urge to answer him.

Maddie was shrieking madly and running about the town square. "It's a thief in my store! A thief!" She continued to run until she had no breath. Maddie collapsed on the brittle dirt-and-stone street.

Ellie slid down a chute that led to Maddie's locked office. Ellie pushed against the door and soon found that she was trapped inside. She called Maddie on her cell, but Maddie had collapsed on the street and couldn't answer.

She tried Annie and Gertie, but Annie was in the middle of a lecture and Gertie was bagging an expensive jar of Paula's Paw Putty. They didn't answer. Ellie sat on Maddie's swivel chair and sulked.

A few minutes later, Gertie opened the door to Maddie's office. "Ellie called to tell me that you're stuck in here miss," Gertie said as Ellie tipped her helmet and dashed away. Gertie turned to Annie. "I love that superhero."

Ellie darted past the stores on the street and followed the thief into the open grasses. There he stopped to catch his breath and look around. Ellie pounced on him. "Don't you dare move a muscle!" she demanded as she slowly got off the disheveled shrew. "Take off your hood."

The thief removed his dark hood and hung his head in shame. Ellie gasped. "Mr. Gourmet?" Mr. Gourmet shrugged. "The food business hasn't paid well. I'm not much of a cook, so I had to hire lots and lots of people to do the work for me. All I do for my company is meet with new employees and make the money. But all those shrews have to get paid."

Ellie couldn't believe it! This guy was a thief? "You didn't employ me, I mean that nice shrew that came by the other day so that you could save yourself some dough, huh," Ellie said. Mr. Gourmet nodded. "I'm sorry. I won't steal anymore."

Ellie shook her head. "Sorry Buster. You gotta talk to Mayor Shrew and Judge Shrew before you can promise anything." She marched him to the mayor's office and shoved him inside before he could protest.

When Ellie came out again, she was her regular self. Maddie, Annie and Gertie folded her into a tight hug. "You missed it!" screamed Maddie. Ellie smiled. "Did I? I feel like I was right there!" The girls looked confused. Ellie sighed. "There's something I haven't told you yet about me, isn't there?"

Maddie, Annie and Gertie shrugged. Ellie laughed. "You three are so gullible! Okay, I'll start with that first day I battled Emerson Eagle. Oh and Annie, you remember your birthday party right? That was me battling the snake. Oh, so much to tell you!"

SNEAK PEAK: SAMANTHA'S SPECIAL SPRING

"It's Sam," I corrected flatly, and then picked up my book bag and headed to my room.

I knew why my dad's date was over at our house. I knew why he even *had* a date in the first place. My mother had died last year of pancreatic cancer. It devastated all of us, my dad especially. But things turned around, for him at least. He met Isabelle at a prayer meeting and recently, they started, well, dating. The engagement ring was on its way, I supposed.

At my little desk, I grabbed my laptop. My social studies binder bulged with homework. I pulled out my Greek vs. Romans worksheet, when I noticed a project assignment tucked in the back.

"Oh great," I groaned. Amelia Jane was good at social studies assignments, but I was better at writing essays for English class. I felt a horrible knot in my stomach. I carefully read the guidelines.

"The guidelines below will help you complete the Diary of a Native American assignment." I read aloud. I skimmed through the guideline pages, and learned that I was to write a diary of a Native American boy or girl from any of the seven tribes we'd learned about. "We've never learned about any Native American tribes, but I can research on it," I said.

This is should be easy, I thought to myself. As I put my binder back into my backpack, a paper scratched me on my left hand. I yanked my hand out suddenly, and a paper fell out of my bag.

I stooped to get it, and saw that it was the sign-up sheet for the school sports teams' spring season. "Soccer's coming back," I said to myself. I looked around my room at the soccer trophies and champion posters.

I slid off swivel chair and went to talk to my dad.

"Isabelle," my dad was saying when I entered the kitchen. "I don't want to move to Scalpel. Hillside Rock is a nice little community nestled in the hills of Pennsylvania. I know you're from Scalpel, Connecticut, and I'm sure it's nice there, but our home is here."

I stole quietly into the kitchen. I don't know how my dad saw me, but he did. "Do you need something Sam?" he asked without turning to face me. I nodded, and brought the sign-up sheet toward him carefully. I cleared my throat, squared my shoulders, and opened my mouth. Thankfully, Isabelle saved me.

"Sports? Is this something you're interested in doing, Sam?" I nodded silently, wondering how she knew that I didn't want to ask my dad to let me join. My dad looked at both of us before saying, "All right Sam. But please come home immediately after practice. Izzy, Max and I will be there for every tryout game."

I thought of my brother Max. He was in high school. *It's not fair,* I thought to myself. *Amelia Jane wants so badly to play basketball, and Max can. And I can play the sports I want to, but she can't.*

"Thanks Daddy," I said, turned sharply on my heels, and headed toward my room.

Make sure you look out for our next book in this series:
SAMANTHA'S SPECIAL SPRING

Made in the USA
Middletown, DE
30 November 2016